BOGUS BEASTS
IN SEARCH OF IMAGINARY ANIMALS

Illustrated by Marc Nadel   Written by Jeff O'Hare

To my mother and father with eternal thanks.

—Marc

For Mom and Dad who started me on this safari—with love.

—Jeff

Published by Bell Books
Boyds Mills Press, Inc.
A Highlights Company
815 Church Street
Honesdale, Pennsylvania 18431
Printed in China

Publisher Cataloging-in-Publication Data

O'Hare, Jeff.
Bogus beasts : in search of imaginary animals / by Jeff O'Hare ;
illustrated by Marc Nadel.
[32]p. : ill. ; cm.
Summary: : A nature book in which children search different
environments and discover imaginary animals.
ISBN 1-56397-812-1
1. Animals—Miscellanea—Juvenile literature. 2. Nature—Miscellanea
—Juvenile literature. 3. Imagination-Juvenile literature.
[1.Animals—Miscellanea. 2. Nature—Miscellanea. 3.Imagination.]
I. Nadel, Marc, ill. II. Title.
590 dc21 1999 AC CIP
Library of Congress Catalog Card Number 99-60223

First edition, 1999
Book designed by Randy Llewellyn
The text of this book is set in Helvetica

10 9 8 7 6 5 4 3 2 1

BOGUS BEASTS

IN SEARCH OF IMAGINARY ANIMALS

This safari takes us in search of fake fauna. *Fauna* is a Latin word meaning "the animals of a certain environment."

All the animals you'll see on each page are real except one. One phony animal, a bogus beast, has managed to sneak into each environment, disrupting the real animals that belong there. It is up to you to determine which is the imaginary animal.

The best way to approach your assignment is to read each animal's description of itself. You must read carefully for clues that will help you pick out which animal doesn't really exist.

Now be very quiet and don't make any sudden moves. This safari begins as soon as you turn the page.

Written by
Jeff O'Hare

Illustrated by
Marc Nadel

Boyds Mills Press

DOLPHINS AND WHALES

Something's fishy, but it isn't these creatures. Dolphins and whales are really mammals. That means they breathe air because, unlike fish, they do not have gills, which can process oxygen right out of the water. Dolphins and whales are very smart. They use echolocation to find food and to identify things in the water. That's what helps them swim so well straight ahead, even though their eyes are off to either side.

Can you find the fake floater?

Bowhead Whale

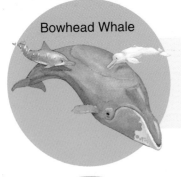

I can grow to be fifty feet long, and one-third of that is just my head. I have twelve-foot-long bristles that hang like a curtain in my mouth, filtering the water for food. If I'm under ice and need to breathe, I just crash through, since I have no dorsal fin that might get injured.

Narwhal

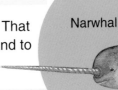

The point of what makes me different is my spectacular spiral spike. That very long tusk is really one of my two teeth. I use it to root out food and to duel with other males.

Strap-Toothed Whale

I won't say much because we males have two teeth that grow up from our lower jaws and curl over our snouts. Eventually this "lip lock" stops us from opening our mouths fully. We manage to eat by sucking water into our mouths and straining out small sea life.

Boutu

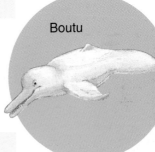

I'm a freshwater dolphin who lives in the Amazon and other rivers, far from the sea. My long beak has whiskers that help me feel my way along muddy waterways. As I get older, my color lightens until I'm a pale, playful pink.

Shevrolay's Dolphin

I am the only family member with two top dorsal fins. This allows me to swim smoothly in open water and still make quick turns around the rocky coasts. My sleek body has no hair at all. Unlike the high clicks and squeals of most dolphins, my voice is a deep honking sound.

Spinner Dolphin

Let's see anyone "top" this! Other dolphins may leap from the water when they breathe, but I'm the only one who spins at the same time. And my dorsal fin has a perfect pyramid profile.

Susu

I, too, am a freshwater dolphin, but I live in India. My river home is so filled with silt that my tiny eyes only sense dark and light. I rely totally on echolocation to find food. As I swim on my side, using my paddle-like fins, I wave my thin snout back and forth until I find lunch.

Beluga

I'm not nicknamed "sea canary" because I'm little and yellow. In fact, I can grow to eighteen feet long, and I have a white color. It's my great variety of whistles and clicks that explains my nickname. I make up for my short snout by having a very flexible neck.

FROGS AND TOADS

Hop to it! With their long, springy back legs, that's the only way to keep up with amphibians. Frogs and toads are at home on land and in water. Most males have throat sacs that they inflate to make croaking sounds. With wide mouths, bulging eyes, and long tongues that shoot out to snare food, you might think all frogs and toads are alike. But don't jump to conclusions.

Can you find the phony frog?

White's Tree Frog

At only four inches long, I'm one of the world's largest tree frogs. However, I get teased about being four inches wide as well. Of course, where I live in dry Australia, being able to hold a lot of water helps you survive.

Hairy Frog

My hairy frills are actually part of my skin. They let me extract oxygen from the rushing water I live in. The retractable needle-sharp claws near my feet keep me anchored so that I am not swept downstream.

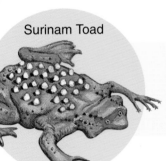

Surinam Toad

All frogs and toads are born from eggs, and I have a built-in "egg carton" on my back. The eggs stay snug among the bumps until the youngsters hatch. My triangular head and wide, webbed feet help me swim, which I do most of my life.

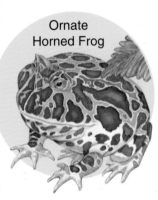

Ornate Horned Frog

With all my fancy markings, you may think I'm a show-off. But I actually spend most of my time buried up to my wide mouth in mud so that I can surprise my prey. And it's always a surprise when a seven-inch, horn-headed, rainbow-blotched frog pops out of the ground!

Poison-Dart Frog

Though I'm a tiny gem of a frog, my skin secretes a very powerful poison! My bright colors are actually a warning to other animals to stay away. The only ones who don't are the native people of tropical America. They coat their blowgun darts with my toxin when they hunt.

Red-Eyed Tree Frog

My eyes are red as a warning to others. If I sense a predator approaching during my daytime rest, my eyes pop open. The enemy is so startled that I can hop out of harm's way. With my suction-cup digits, my landings are secure.

Elephant Toad

Unlike my relatives, I don't catch insects with a long sticky tongue. My camouflage markings help me to sneak up on a meal, as I patiently wait for the right moment. When I pounce, my unique, powerful tusks make short work of even the toughest bug.

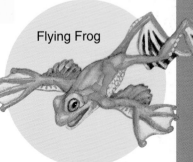

Flying Frog

I just flew in from Borneo, and, boy, are my webbed feet tired! Actually, I don't fly, but glide from one tree to another. I use my widely webbed and fringed hands and feet as parachutes. Of course, I'm used to high living, since I started life in a cloud-like foam nest in the trees.

MONKEYS AND APES

Primates are some of the smartest mammals on earth. Those from tropical America are generally small tree dwellers with prehensile, or grasping, tails. The rest are Old World monkeys from Africa and Asia. These include larger animals, including apes with no tails at all.

It's up to you to expose the pretend primate.

Proboscis Monkey

Is that my nose or am I eating a banana? Actually, it is my nose, and I have to move it when I eat. It naturally amplifies my danger call into an incredibly loud "honk." This allows normal-nosed females and the young to escape into the Borneo jungle or to dive into water and swim to safety.

White Uakari

Boy, is my face red! But that doesn't mean I'm embarrassed. It means I'm healthy! Of all the New World monkeys, I'm the only one with a stubby tail and a bald head. But when I leap from a high branch and let my long fur stream out behind me, I think I look beautiful.

Emperor Tamarin

No other monkeys have a wide white moustache, and that's a big problem. The moustache makes it easy for predators, such as eagles, to spot me. I've had to develop some speedy zigzag movements for quick getaways. The danger from human collectors, however, is not so easy to escape.

Mandrill

With my blue-ridged cheeks, red nose and muzzle, and orange collar, it's like Halloween every day. I'm a scary-looking creature with long canine teeth and a weight of 100 pounds. The largest of all monkeys, I live in large troops that mostly stay on the ground.

Wow-Wow

That's what I'm called in Java, and it's what you would say if you saw me swinging high in the jungle. I'm also known as the Silvery Gibbon, one of the ape family that has incredibly long arms and fingers. These allow me to cover forty-five feet in one swooping, swift swing.

Yakisaki

Listen here! I am the only primate who can imitate other animals. I am slow moving for a monkey, so I use my vocal talent to fool predators. If I see a hawk, for instance, I might scare it off by imitating a jaguar.

Spider Monkey

My tale is about my tail. I use it to hang from branches, to swing to other trees, or even to pick up objects like fruit. In Brazil, you can see my acrobatic stunts, such as leaping from a branch backward or dropping upside down and flipping over to land safely.

Golden Snub-Nosed Monkey

I live high in the same Chinese mountains as the giant panda. That means I have to deal with snow and other winter conditions, and eat lichen to survive. I travel far to find food, and when spring comes, our troops begin to eat leaves. Our survival is most threatened, however, by fellow primates—human poachers.

WILD FOWL
This large family includes pheasants, quails, and grouse. They live all over the world. The males perform very fancy dancing displays, using bright puffed-up feathers, loud noises, and wing thumping. The one who's most impressive is chosen by females.

Can you flush out the fake fowl?

Temminck's Tragopan

For my delightful display, I find a clearing, hide behind a rock, and call out to attract females. When they arrive, I suddenly poke my head above the rock, showing my horns and spectacular inflated "bib." Then I cluck, stand on tiptoes, puff out my feathers, shake my head, and circle the female. My show can be seen in Eastern Asia.

Black-Eyed Peafowl

I'm usually found in the southern United States. I'm the only pheasant with long, webbed toes, which allow me to scoot along the surface of swampy areas. My name doesn't come from my eyes, which are actually brown. My tail feathers and crest, however, have black, eye-like markings.

Spruce Grouse

In America's evergreen forests each spring, I perform my own special display. I fly up to low branches and down again, enlarge my red eyebrows, then drag my wings, spread my tail, and dance. Afterward, I thump my wings repeatedly against my sides to create a loud drumming sound.

Unlike my cousin peacock, my tail doesn't spread out into a great fan of feathers with eye-like spots. But my wings do! My two tail feathers are four feet long, so I can wiggle them over the top of my outstretched wings. I'm named for Argus, a Greek mythical giant who had 100 eyes.

Great Argus

Bulwer's Wattled Pheasant

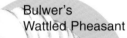

I'm the wild bird of Borneo. With my back to a female, I show off my cloud-like white tail and ground-scratching quills. Then I turn around quickly and startle her with my red eye-rings surrounded by bright blue horns and beard-like wattles. Pretty wild!

Willow Ptarmigan

I may be Alaska's state bird, but don't expect to spot me there. Although my feathers match the brown tundra all summer, each winter I turn snow white. I'm quite at home in the snow, with feathered snowshoes and claws to dig out snow chambers for shelter. I choose a mate for life, and fiercely defend her and our eggs from predators.

Painted Quail

I am so small that I can easily fit into a person's palm. In fact, in ancient China, my homeland, we actually were used as hand warmers. A much more natural activity for us is leading our tiny, fluffy chicks around in parade fashion. Isn't that heartwarming?

Actually, I'm a grouse, and definitely not chicken! In fact, we males challenge each other as part of our display dance. At dawn, in early spring, we lower our heads, raise our tails, inflate our big orange throat sacs, and put our feathered horns up. Then we stamp our feet, rush forward, leap, and hoot. And all this before breakfast!

Greater Prairie Chicken

HOOFED AND HORNED MAMMALS
This wide-spread family lives in vastly different climates and has vastly different appearances. Some are goats, some are antelopes, and some are just plain odd! Their hooves, however, are all even-toed, with two points apiece. The horns can be long, short, curved, straight, smooth, or rough.
Can you detect the hoofed hypocrite?

Klipspringer

With my two cone-shaped horns, sunburst ears and round, dark nose surrounded by a white muzzle, I look like a clown. But I'm actually an acrobat! I live in rocky areas in Africa, and jump from peak to peak. My hooves are small and round enough to let me land on a rocky ledge only inches wide.

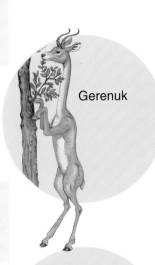
Gerenuk

Although I look like a little giraffe, I'm really a type of gazelle. With long legs and neck, I'm able to reach some high leaves in my dry African home. But when those leaves are finished, I reach even higher by standing on my hind legs. Then I just walk around the tree, having dessert.

Saiga

Scientists say I'm a goat-antelope, but I don't look like either. My muzzle is funny looking, but very useful. My Russian steppe home is cold and dry, so my nose heats up to dampen the air I breathe. If the air becomes too dry, my nose can locate moisture and lead me to a drink.

Dik-Dik

I may be only a fourteen-inch-tall antelope, but my leaping ability is among the greatest of all mammals. When startled, I call out my name and, without bending my legs, pop up like a mechanical toy. Then I leap away with blazing speed. My flexible snout helps me reach leaves that are over my head.

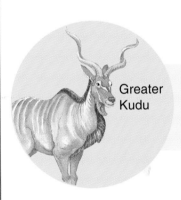
Greater Kudu

I really am great! No other antelope combines white stripes and facial markings, shoulder and throat manes, large size, and, above all, a magnificent set of curled horns. Even with these four-foot twisters, I'm still able to leap six feet into the air.

Golden Takin

I come from remote, rocky, and rugged mountains in China. Takins are not closely related to any other animals, but you could guess that just by looking at us. I have a beautiful golden coat, a big bulbous muzzle, too-small horns, sleepy eyes, and a huge body.

Sawbuck

I am named for the ten sharp little ridges on my horns. I use them like a saw's teeth and cut down thin, high branches with tasty leaves, which I normally couldn't reach. In order to blend into the tall grass of the African savannah, my fur has a coating of algae, which gives me a green back.

Markhor

I am a wild goat of the high mountains of Pakistan, which means I need to be a very sure-footed leaper and climber. I'm three feet high at the shoulder, but that's where I stop being a typical goat. My foot-long beard is dwarfed by my magnificent five-foot-long corkscrew horns.

TURTLES AND TORTOISES
People have had mobile homes for decades, but these reptiles have had them for millions of years. Deserts, jungles, rocky ledges, and even oceans are all places where these creatures might show their faces.

It's up to you to spot the shell shocker.

Pancake Tortoise

Flat is where it's at! I live in rocky areas where there are plenty of crevices. At the first sign of danger, I race to one of the cracks. Thanks to my special flattened shell, I can crawl between the two rocks, lift myself on short, powerful legs, and wedge myself in until the danger has passed.

Matamata

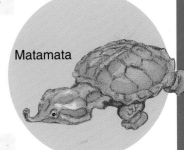

I may be the weirdest looking of all turtles, but that's because I'm part scuba diver, part vacuum cleaner. As I hide in murky, shallow water, I breathe through my snorkel snout. When I sense the vibration of a fish, I move my strong neck side to side, open my mouth, and vacuum in my meal.

Big-Headed Turtle

What a bonehead! My head is too big to fit into any shell, but since it's protected by bony armor, there's no problem. My tail is armored and big too, almost half of my twelve-inch length. I use it, along with my long claws, to climb trees in mountainous Southeast Asia.

Wing-Ding Turtle

My top shell, or carapace, looks dull in water, but not if I'm on dry land. Then my special flair can be seen. My shell has wide flanges on the sides, which allow me to skip across a lake's surface like a stone. Then I open my mouth and skim the water for small fish while making a loud whistling sound.

Leatherback Turtle

Measuring six feet in length and weighing half a ton, I am the world's largest turtle. In most oceans, I can be found eating jellyfish. The females of our species come ashore to lay eggs on sandy beaches. My life in cold ocean water is eased by being able to raise my body heat slightly. That's unique in reptiles, and so is my football-shaped shell.

Alligator Snapping Turtle

I love to fish. When I open my mouth, you can see a little wormlike lure on my tongue that wiggles in the water. When an unsuspecting fish tries to eat it . . . SNAP! My powerful jaws close like a trap, and I have dinner. But I'm called "Alligator" because of my ridged and pointy top shell looks like a gator's back.

Eastern Box Turtle

Safety is very important to me, and with my special shell I'm perfectly safe! My plastron, or bottom shell, has a special hinge. When I'm in danger, I pull in my head, legs, and tail, then use the hinge to lock myself in.

Galapagos Tortoise

As the biggest land turtle, at 500 pounds and five feet long, I spend a lot of time eating plants. Of course, I have a lot of time because my lifespan is the longest of all animals. On my South American island home, I can live to be 150 years old!

BATS
Bats are the only mammals that truly fly. Their wings are thin membranes stretched like an umbrella over elongated finger bones. Many bats fly at night, eating insect pests. Bats target the bugs by emitting hundreds of ultrasonic sonar clicks per second! These hit the insects and echo back to the bats' large ears to let them know the location of a meal. Other bats are fruit eaters who help trees by spreading pollen and seeds.

Can you identify the false flapper?

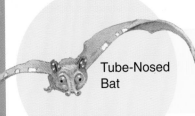

Tube-Nosed Bat

I'm one bat with good vision, thanks to my large orange eyes. But it's my nose that's really special. The tubes keep liquid out of my nose when I eat fruit, and keep dusty pollen out when I drink nectar. You can find me in Indonesia and other Pacific islands.

Townsend's Big-Eared Bat

I have the greatest sonar receivers of all. My ears are half as long as my whole four-inch body. When I rest, I can curl them up like a ram's horns. I'm awake at night, when I catch moths in a pocket stretched between my legs.

Louisville Sluggish Bat

I'm the world's laziest bat. I chase after prey by flying back and forth in an arc, hoping to make contact. I usually try three times and then rest. I hibernate all winter, then return to my old Kentucky orchard home each spring.

White Bat

My leaf-shaped nose fine-tunes my sonar as I navigate through the tropical South American rain forest. At three inches long, it's easy to hide in coconut palm trees, which is lucky because, otherwise, my snow-white coat would make me an easy target for predators.

Bonnet Bat

I got my name because my big ears join at the base, fall over my forehead, and reach way down the sides of my face. I'm seven inches long, with a long tail that helps me feel my way through narrow cave crevices. My loud cries sound scary, especially to the grasshoppers and crickets I eat.

Flying Fox

I'm one of the world's largest bats, twelve inches long, with a wingspread of more than four feet! My name is based on my long, pointy muzzle, which I use to gobble up fruit. I live in Southeast Asia, and gather in large groups to rest in trees near water. Since I eat and sleep in trees, I'm a great pollinator of seeds.

Hammerhead Bat

Among bats, only I have small ears, big eyes, and a large muzzle. My notable nose amplifies my honking voice so that a faraway female can find me. When she arrives, she chooses the loudest male as a mate. I'm Africa's largest bat and can grow to ten and one-half inches in length.

Fishing Bat

I use my ears as sonar detectors like other bats, but there are no moths on my menu. I like fish! I skim over a lake and listen for rippling water where fish are feeding. Then I drop my large clawed feet below the surface and hook my meal. As I fly higher, I swing the fish up into my mouth.

INSECT-EATING MAMMALS
These anteaters, armadillos, and pangolins are among the oddest-looking animals. They share certain traits, particularly their favorite food and how they get it. Using strong claws to break open the nests of ants and termites, they gobble them up with long, thin, shooting, sticky tongues.
Can you expose the artificial ant chomper?

Giant Anteater

You can see me in the grasslands of Central and South America. In fact, you can hardly miss me! I'm eight feet long and have a huge tail that helps shade me from the sun. I rip open rock-hard termite mounds with my huge claws, and lap up meals by shooting out my sticky twelve-inch tongue.

Fairy Armadillo

I'm only six inches long, with pink armor on my back, white fur underneath my body and on my face, and a spoon-shaped tail. I live in a burrow, and I dig like a mole. I live only in the dry plains of Argentina, and I'm very rare. To survive, I need human help and, maybe, some fairy dust.

Indian Pangolin

Though we look alike, I'm no armadillo. I'm armored, and each of my scales is very sharp. If threatened, I curl into a spiral and hook my tail onto my back. I have no teeth, and shoot out my sticky tongue to gather up insects. Pangolins also live in China, Malaysia, and Africa.

I use my prehensile tail to get around the treetops of the tropical rainforest. At night, my sense of smell helps me find ants under bark. My specialized large claw, like a can opener, rips open the branch, and then I dine! Although only one foot long, I can eat 3,000 ants in one day. My soft, fluffy fur is dense enough to protect me from getting bitten.

Silky Anteater

Tamandua

I'm the second largest anteater. I spend my time in trees, looking for ants and termites. With my prehensile tail and long tongue, I can reach almost anywhere. If caught on the ground, I will stand on my back legs and try to "hug" my enemy with powerful arms and very sharp claws.

While other anteaters have prehensile tails, mine also has an elastic quality. If threatened while I'm on a branch, I wrap my tail around it, curl up my body, and jump off. The predator thinks I've fallen, and when it leaves, I just pull myself back up! I have a low, musical voice.

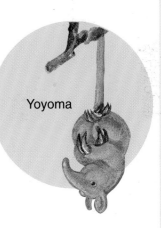

Yoyoma

Bola

My name is Spanish for "ball." When I'm threatened, I roll into a perfect, armored ball until my enemy leaves. I'm the only armadillo who can do this. My armor has three bands with a special notch, where I tuck my head and tail like jigsaw puzzle pieces. My home is the hottest region of South America.

I'm a five-foot-long, 120-pound living steam shovel with a specialized eight-inch curved claw on each front paw. I have been known to dig through concrete and toss it aside! I can walk on my hind legs, and I use my 100 teeth to grind tough insects. I live near rivers in the Amazon rain forest.

Giant Armadillo

NORTH AMERICAN DUCKS
If it waddles like a duck, quacks like a duck, has a flattened bill, webbed feet and is at home on the water, and especially if it's on these pages, it's a duck! (All except the one "quack," of course!) The males pictured here are shown in their fanciest breeding feathers.
Ready to identify the deceptive duck?

Surf Scooter

My silly looks have given me nicknames like "Gogglenose" and "Skunk Duck." But I'm actually a rugged sea duck, riding the waves in rough weather. I can dive forty feet to get my favorite food, shellfish. I just swallow them whole, crushing the shell in my gizzard.

Ruddy Duck

You've never seen another duck like me. From my bright blue bill to my spikey fan tail, I'm different. My legs are so short and so far back that I can barely walk on land. I even have to paddle and skip across water before I'm moving fast enough to fly. Females lay up to ten big eggs, which is a lot for a little duck.

Common Eider

Get down! That's not a warning or an invitation to dance. I'm talking about my incredibly warm inner layer of little feathers. Females use it to line nests to warm our eggs. When our ducklings hatch, they follow their mother through the woods to the sea. I'm very large for a duck, and can grow to more than two feet long.

My white crest can be raised and lowered like a fan. All Mergansers' bills are unlike those of other ducks. Our bills are thin and pointed. We have sawlike "teeth" with a hook on the tip so that when we dive, we can hold on to our fish dinner. We sometimes share nest sites with wood ducks, and take turns incubating the eggs.

Hooded Merganser

Lookout Duck

I have the sharpest eyesight of all ducks, and I swim around the edges of flocks of my cousins. If danger is lurking, I warn the others with a wing-flapping, water-spraying, quacking display. As the others scatter, I put my head down, because that's when I have to duck and "look out."

I may have a white belly, but I'm no sapsucker. I nest near rivers and forest streams, often in tree holes fifty feet high. When our dozen ducklings hatch, they either climb down (using beak and foot hooks), flutter down, or are carried down by their mother.

Wood Duck

Barrow's Goldeneye

With my purple feathers, white crescent, and, of course, golden eye, my head looks like a night sky. Actually, I'm very active all day long, as I enjoy shooting rapids. I will even swim over a little waterfall and pop up at the bottom. Each spring, males swim around females, throw their heads way back, point their bills to the sky, and whistle and click.

Other ducks may be prettier, larger, or faster, but only I have such a long spoon-shaped bill. As I swim in shallow water, I wave my beak underwater, probing for little bits of food. My bill has special little strainers on each side so that water drains off when I bring it above the surface.

Northern Shoveler

LIZARDS
Of all reptiles, lizards have the widest variety of sizes, shapes, colors, and habitats. Most have a tail and four legs, but there are species who look like snakes. However, they all hatch from eggs and have movable eyelids, and they are all cold-blooded. Many are colored to blend with their backgrounds, and chameleons can actually change color to completely camouflage themselves.
    Can you locate the lying lizard?

Jackson's Chameleon

Now you see me, now you don't! Like a mini-triceratops, I have three horns and a bony crest which protect my neck. I can also move each eye separately for protection and hunting. I can grasp branches with my prehensile tail, and catch bugs with my long, sticky tongue.

Piebald Piguana

How did I get such a funny name? Well, *piebald* doesn't mean I have dessert on my bare head; it means "spotted." And *piguana* comes from the fact that I snort, I'm round, and I have a curly little tail. I also have a huge appetite for insects, and help control their numbers in my swampy home in Central America.

Gliding Gecko

I come from Southeast Asia, and never go anywhere without my parachute. I have special flaps of skin on my sides and tail, and widely webbed feet. They allow me to sail from one branch to another. All geckos have specialized feet. With both bristly hooks and suction cup-like feet, we can cling to any surface, even upside down. I can grow to eight inches long, head to fringed tail.

Surprise! When I'm startled, I open my wide mouth and unfold a huge fan-shaped collar. This is usually enough to startle an enemy. But just in case, I have one more trick. I can get up on my hind legs and run away, looking like a bow-legged man with an umbrella.

Australian Frilled Lizard

Gila Monster

I may be covered with a pretty pattern of black and coral beads, but I'm no beanbag. In fact, I'm one of the world's few venomous lizards. I live in United States and Mexican deserts and store fat in my tail. That way, if I can't find food or water, I can survive for months. I'm less than twenty inches long, but my bite is a big pain.

Basilisk

I only live in trees that overhang a river so that I can dive in in case of danger. Sometimes I swim down and stay under for a while. But other times, I pop back up and—believe it or not—I stand up and run across the surface of the water! I don't sink because of my long fringed widespread toes, my light weight, and my dazzling speed.

Komodo Dragon

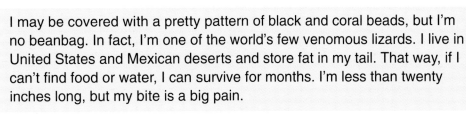

Measuring ten feet long and weighing 350 pounds, I'm the world's largest lizard. My home is Indonesia, where I'll eat animals as large as deer. I use my long tail as a weapon and my long forked tongue as a sensing device. Unlike most lizards, my neck allows my head to turn in many directions, which makes me even more dangerous.

Moloch

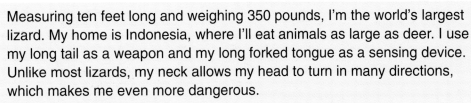

I'm a small lizard from the Australian desert, and I'm known as the thorny devil. You can see why! My body is covered in spikes of different sizes, especially around my head. I even have a spiked ball on my neck for extra protection. Ants could use protection from me because I can eat up to 1,000 of them in just one meal.

PARROTS
For many parrots, talk is more than "cheep." With an ability to mimic most sounds, they can imitate people, animals, machines, and other birds. Of course, they use their big beaks for many other purposes, including cracking nuts, climbing trees, and even pulling up tasty roots like a shovel.
Can you identify the fine-feathered phony?

Major Mitchell's Cockatoo

I'm tickled pink to show off my magnificent flame-like crest! Cockatoos are mid-size parrots who live in Australia and the Pacific islands. Most can raise their crests, but only mine is red and orange. We're good talkers, which helps when we return with our life-long mates to the same nesting hole each year.

Kakapo

I don't look or act like my parrot cousins. In New Zealand, I'm active at night and sleep during the day. I'm flightless, although I can glide, waddle along, and climb trees. By trimming grass with my beak, I make paths between feeding areas and resting places. There are very few of us left, and we need human help to survive.

Purple Polar Parrot

Of all parrots, I'm the only one to inhabit cold Antarctic islands. To keep warm, I've developed a double layer of feathers for insulation. Since there are no nuts or fruits available, I have a different diet. I use my powerful beak to pry open oysters and clams for a seafood dinner.

Are you talking to me? Because I'm talking to you! I'm one of the best talkers of all parrots. Beyond that, scientists have discovered that we are quite intelligent, and that we understand much of what we're saying. (I could have told them that!)

African Grey Parrot

Scarlet Macaw

Macaws are the largest parrots, and I'm a full three feet long, including my magnificent tail. My powerful bill can crack the hardest nuts, and when I'm climbing, it can grip any branch. The white part of my face has no feathers on it so that when I eat fruit, I don't get all sticky.

Most people think all parrots have an Amazon's green body, curved hook beak, square tail, and talking ability. Our feet are especially adapted and we use them like hands to hold food when we eat. While all the Amazons have touches of color, only I have a full yellow head.

Yellow-Headed Amazon

Hawk-Headed Parrot

While the cockatoos have crests that rise up like fins, I have my own style. When I get excited or angry, I have a halo of feathers that opens up like a fan. Though I'm called "Hawk," I eat only fruit and nuts in my Amazon rain forest home.

Lories are among the most colorful creatures in the world, but I outdo even my cousins. My fabulous feathers are just one of my special features. Like other lories, I love flower nectar and pollen. So, in order to collect them, I've developed a little brush on the tip of my tongue. I actually brush during every meal!

Rainbow Lorikeet

PROSIMIANS
These are primates, like monkeys and apes, but are much more primitive animals. In general, their hands are not as human-like, and their brains are not as sophisticated. Unlike almost all monkeys, many prosimians are nocturnal. They live in isolated areas of Africa and Asia, and thrive on islands where they don't have to compete with their primate cousins.

It's up to you to pick out the preposterous prosimian.

Tarsier

My big bat-like ears and big owl-like eyes tell you I'm a night creature. Also, like an owl, I can swivel my head around far enough to prevent an enemy from sneaking up behind me. I live on Asian islands. I'm named for my long ankle bones, which help me leap. My tail, twice as long as my five-inch body, acts as a rudder. I land securely, using suction-cuplike fingers and toes.

Indri

Three feet tall, I am the biggest lemur, and the only one without a tail. In the treetops, however, I am difficult to see because of my coat's dark and light pattern. My long hands and feet make me a great climber, and my long legs let me leap up to twenty feet to another branch. All lemurs live on Madagascar, an island off Africa's eastern coast.

Fat-Tailed Dwarf Lemur

I live in very dry areas of Madagascar where I can't always find water. That's when my balloon-like tail comes into play. When food and water are available, I fill up my tail like a nutrient-storage tank. Then, when necessary, I can hibernate for several weeks, living off the fat of the tail.

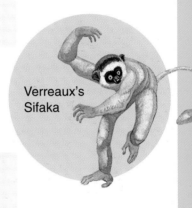

Verreaux's Sifaka

Like most lemurs, I spend much of my life in treetops. But when a Sifaka comes down to the ground, it moves like no other animal. I stand up on my long legs, stretch out my short arms, and using my long furry tail as a balance, I bounce along sideways. And then I'm going-boing-gone!

Ring-Tailed Lemur

Unlike most prosimians, I spend most of my time on the ground, along with about thirty other troop members. I walk on all fours with my raccoon-like tails up to let the others know where I am. My tail is longer than my body and helps me balance and steer. Active during the day, I always hoot before I go to sleep, to tell the others my location.

Potto

I may look cute and cuddly, but don't touch! When threatened, I lower my head to reveal sharp horns on the back of my neck. My hands and feet have extra long thumbs and short index fingers to give me a powerful grip. Our babies hold onto their mother's belly for their first month, and have white fur for six months. I live in African jungle treetops.

Slender Loris

I'm a creeper, not a leaper. In India and Sri Lanka, I use just my thick arms and legs to crawl along branches at night (I have no tail). Only eight inches long, I hunt grasshoppers. When I see one, I turn on the speed and pounce. Then it's back to life in the slow lane, as I wrap myself around a branch to rest.

Boffo

I'm a natural show-off who does everything in a big way! We males have attention-getting reddish fur and white ear tufts. But my swiftly swirling tail and loud, laughing call warn competitors to stay back. I then perform acrobatic swings and leaps, and wait for the birds to pop out.

OCEAN FISH

Of all the world's animals, fish have the most bizarre shapes, spectacular colors, and special abilities. They breathe with gills, swim with fins, and have scales. They are sometimes called "bony" fish to separate them from jellyfish (with no skeletons) or crawfish (with external skeletons). Actually, neither of those is a true fish at all!

It's up to you to find the fake fish.

Leafy Sea Dragon

When I hide near a kelp bed off the coast of Australia, you would think I'm just another strand of seaweed. I certainly fool both predators and my favorite food, tiny shrimp, which I inhale with my snout. As a male, I incubate eggs given to me by a female, until they hatch. Then I'm a proud dragon dad!

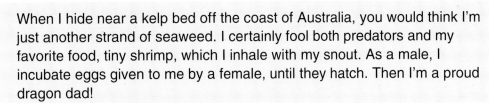

Pufferfish

I may look cute, but I'm actually a triple threat! First, I'm covered with tiny sharp spikes. Second, when threatened, I can inflate into this large balloon so enemies can't eat me. And last, but not least, my skin and organs are very poisonous! So remember, no cuddling.

Icebreaker Fish

My favorite food, microscopic krill, live in the coldest waters of the Arctic. The bony wedge on my forehead can produce enough heat to melt thin layers of ice. When that doesn't reach my prey, I use the wedge as an ice pick, to break off chunks and clear the way. The natives of this region use me as an offering to begin conversations.

I live a mile below the ocean surface. Since sunlight never reaches that far down, I provide my own light. The first spike on my back fin has become a long fishing rod with a fleshy light bulb on its tip. Bacteria produce the light. It hangs from my forehead in front of my mouth and attracts prey. We six-inch females are twenty-five times bigger than males!

Deep-Sea Angler Fish

Mola

I'm eight feet long and I weigh two tons, but my tail fin is so small it looks as if it's been cut off. Although I'm the world's heaviest bony fish, I'm a gentle creature who eats only little jellyfish. I'm also called ocean sunfish because I sometimes lie on my side on the surface, absorbing the sun's warm rays.

I don't just leap from the water; I actually soar like a glider! If threatened, I speed underwater for forty feet and vibrate my tail like a propeller. Then I break the surface, spread my two sets of fins like wings, and soar up to thirty feet high and a distance of 100 yards. I can also repeat the flight several times and turn in midair to fool predators.

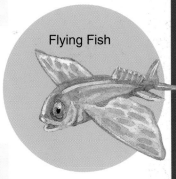

Flying Fish

Cowfish

My strange body shape is protected by a bony case. The armor, however, keeps my body so rigid that I can't bend like other fish. I swim by swinging my short tailfins side to side, which springs me forward in short bursts. My name comes from the "horns" on my forehead. Of course, no one's ever seen a ten-inch yellow cow!

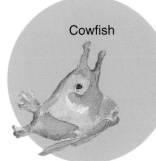

With my spectacular backfin, my sensational spear for a prow, and my two-pointed tail for a rudder, I can move through the sea like a streamlined sailboat. I use my spear as a weapon when necessary, and make powerful, graceful leaps far above the ocean's surface.

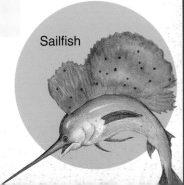

Sailfish

BEARS

Bears are the largest meat eaters, but their diets include everything from ants to bamboo. Their heads and ears are rounds, and they have short tails. Most have small eyes with weak vision, but all bears have great senses of smell and hearing.

It's up to you to unmask the unreal ursine.

Sun Bear

I am the world's smallest bear, weighing less than 140 pounds. But I can be very aggressive, which is important because I'm often hunted by poachers. I live in Asia's tropical rain forests, and to keep cool, I have short fur. As cubs, we hum happily as we suck our paws, the way human children suck their thumbs.

Moon Bear

When I climb a tree in Asia to eat nuts, branches are crushed and gathered beneath me, forming a huge nest. Sometimes, I'll actually sleep in one, but I'm not called moon bear because of my sky-high bed. The name comes from my chest's white crescent. I can walk on my hind legs for a quarter-mile, but at 400 pounds, I can be so round that I roll downhill for fun.

Polar Bear

My home is the icy Arctic. I'm a powerful swimmer and diver who can stay underwater for up to two minutes. My white coat blends against the snow, so that I can surprise seals. It also insulates me by transmitting heat from the sun to my black skin underneath.

Spotted Bear

I can be "spotted" in the densest jungles of Central Africa, and am the only bear on the whole continent. My tawny coat with brown spots helps me blend into the background like a leopard, and I make nests out of leaves like a gorilla. But when it comes to eating fish and berries, I'm all bear.

Spectacled Bear

My name comes from the light markings around my eyes, which look like glasses. I am South America's only bear and live in the Andes Mountains. I weigh less than 400 pounds, and eat mostly vegetation and fruit. Perhaps that's why I spend more time in trees than any other bear. There are only about 2,000 of us left.

Sloth Bear

When British scientists first saw us in Asia 200 years ago, they thought we were giant sloths. I have shaggy fur, long curved sharp claws, and a remarkably long flexible snout. I can close my nostrils, and I have no front teeth. Why? So that when I rip apart termite mounds and anthills, I can vacuum up my favorite insect meals.

Kodiak Bear

You may know grizzlies as North America's huge, powerful, 900-pounders. Now, imagine the same animal weighing twice that much and you've got me! I live in Alaska's Kodiak Islands, away from other bears. There's nothing I like to do more than stand in a rushing stream and catch (and eat) salmon!

Giant Panda

Who's black and white and a bear all over? Me! In recent years, scientists have finally proven that I am a true bear. I'm China's bamboo-eating treasure. I hold my favorite food in my paw with an extra long wrist bone acting like a thumb. There are fewer than 900 of us left, and we need people to protect us and our habitat.

ANSWER KEY These are the bogus beasts.

 Shevrolay's Dolphin

Dolphins and Whales (pages 4-5)

 Elephant Toad

Frogs and Toads (pages 6-7)

 Yakisaki

Monkeys and Apes (pages 8-9)

Wild Fowl (pages 10-11)  Black-Eyed Peafowl

 Sawbuck

Hoofed and Horned Mammals (pages 12-13)

Turtles and Tortoises (pages 14-15)  Wing-Ding Turtle

 Louisville Sluggish Bat

Bats (pages 16-17)

Insect-Eating Mammals (pages 18-19)  Yoyoma

 Lookout Duck

North American Ducks (pages 20-21)

Lizards (pages 22-23)  Piebald Piguana

 Purple Polar Parrot

Parrots (pages 24-25)

Prosimians (pages 26-27)  Boffo

 Icebreaker Fish

Ocean Fish (pages 28-29)

Bears (pages 30-31)  Spotted Bear